PEPPERMINT TEA AND NOTHING IS FREE

Cauldron Coffee Shop

Book 3

LAURA GREENWOOD

Visit Laura Greenwood's website at:

www.authorlauragreenwood.co.uk

Cover by Vampari Designs

Peppermint Tea And Nothing Is Free is a work of fiction. Names, characters, places, and incidents are the products of the author's imagination or are used fictitiously. Any resemblance to actual persons, living or dead, businesses, companies, events, or locales is entirely coincidental.

If you find an error, you can report it via my website. Please note that my books are written in British English: https://www.authorlauragreenwood.co.uk/p/report-error.html

To keep up to date with new releases, sales, and other updates, you can join my mailing list via my website or The Paranormal Council Reader Group on Facebook.

Blurb

**Azíl takes on the modern world,
what could possibly go wrong?**

With Azíl now severed from his teapot,
Willow faces the biggest challenge of
them all...teaching him how to be
human in the modern world.

While their friends and allies have
grown in number, Willow can't forget
that their enemies are out there, and
that they're determined to reinforce the
curse on Azíl and force him back into
his teapot.

And with her heart on the line, she's
determined not to let that happen.

-

Peppermint Tea and Nothing is Free is book three of the Cauldron Coffee Shop Series, a cozy urban fantasy featuring a coffee-shop-owning witch, an ancient warlock cursed to live in a teapot, and a cheeky cat. It includes an m/f romantic subplot.

If you love cozy urban fantasy, coffee shop settings, low-stakes adventures, cat familiars, and a warm and fuzzy feeling vibe, start the Cauldron Coffee Shops series with Pumpkin Spice And All Things Nice.

What Happened
Before

Hazelnut Latte And Something To Say

With Willow having lost a barista thanks to her previous one trying to use blood magic on her, Azíl has been trying to do the job, but quickly finds himself overwhelmed by the outside world, but getting better at it with every day. They also continue their research into the curse that might be inflicting Azíl.

On Sabine's insistence, Willow and Azíl go out for a walk, introducing him to ice cream for the first time, as well as conventional dating rules - which he's been trying to learn about through a game show run by cupids.

Willow and Azíl go to the opening for Sabine's dig finds and are introduced to Mona (from Grimalkin Academy), a curse breaker who Sabine thinks can help with Azíl's situation. Sabine catches Willow and Azíl kissing.

Mona and her friend Daphne come to the coffee shop and say they'll need to study the teapot and will have to take it away from the coffee shop to do as much. They tell Azíl that they can perform a sever spell that will cut his ties to the teapot but not break his curse. He asks to think about it.

Sabine comes to the coffee shop and talks to Willow about the status of her relationship with Azíl and if she's thought things through. In the end, she approves, but says that Willow should be careful.

Azíl agrees to the sever spell, which is performed by Mona, Daphne, and Willow. It successfully separates him from the teapot. He and Willow return upstairs to her apartment where they realise that he now needs somewhere to sleep, at which point Willow suggests that he stays in her room and the two of them sleep together for the first time.

You can find the What Happened Before for book one on my website: https://www.authorlauragreenwood. co.uk/p/what-happened-before-caul dron-coffee.html

Chapter 1

A stream of curses in a language I don't understand comes from the bathroom. I shake my head in slight amusement. I may not know *exactly* what Azíl is saying, but I get the gist of it.

I take a sip of my coffee and set it down on the side before heading over to the site of Azíl's current battle with the modern world.

I knock on the door, not wanting to walk in on anything he doesn't want to see. "Can I come in?" I ask.

"You may," he responds.

I push open the door and stop in my tracks as I take in the three-thousand-year-old warlock standing and glaring at the beard trimmer in his hand.

"What happened?" I ask, trying to keep my attention away from his bare chest. Not that he'll mind me staring, but it's a distraction from the issue at hand.

He lets out a loud sigh. "I do not know how to use it."

"You should have let me get the antique-style razor," I say as I take it from him. "Sit down." I gesture to the edge of the bath.

He does as I ask and I step closer. "Hold still."

"Do you know what you are doing?" he asks.

"No, but I'm going to watch a tutorial." I pull my phone out of my pocket and click through to the video app, grateful that it only takes a few minutes for me to get the right thing.

"What is that?"

"Someone videoed themselves

using a beard trimmer and posted it online." I show him the screen.

"Why?"

The expression on his face is adorable, and fills me with a surge of affection for him. "To help people who don't know how to do it. You can find them for just about anything."

"Anything?" The way he raises his eyebrow lets me know exactly where his thoughts have strayed.

I chuckle. "Probably. But I can assure you that you don't need any tutorials in that department." I step closer. "How long do you want your beard to be?"

He touches it, as if trying to work out the answer to my question. "How long should it be?"

"It's up to you," I point out. "It's your beard."

"But what do you like?" he asks.

"I like this," I admit, reaching out and cupping his cheek in my hand. "I think it suits you."

His responding smile makes my heart skip a beat. "Very well. We shall keep it the same," he says decisively. "I can change my mind at a future date, yes?"

"Any time."

He nods. "I thought as much. I see men with many different styles. Some do not wear a beard at all."

"That's what a lot of people choose now," I say.

"Personal choice," he muses. "You say that about a lot of things."

"Because it's true. Now hold still." I flick the button of the trimmers on and follow the instructions from the video, finding it surprisingly easy to follow. I expected a bit more of a challenge after Azíl's struggles, but that's probably been caused by his lack of knowledge about the modern world. He's learning quickly, but I imagine it's still a confusing experience for him.

The bathroom falls silent save for the slight buzz of the clippers and the soft sound of our breathing. There's something strangely intimate about the situation, probably because I've never done this for anyone before, and I doubt Azíl has been on the receiving end either.

"There," I say, stepping back and setting the clippers down. "Do you have some beard oil?"

He nods. "I believe it is in the box."

I search and find one of them and hand it to him.

"Thank you." He unstoppers the bottle and spreads the oil through his beard, the scent of sandalwood filling the room as a result. It's a nice smell, and one I've come to associate with him now he's got a proper human form again. I guess this is why.

"I'll leave you to get dressed. Do you want breakfast?"

"I would."

"I'll have it ready for you." I lean in and kiss his cheek, enjoying the casual affection more than I ever expected to. I've dated before, but I haven't shared my living space with someone the way I do with Azíl. It's a different kind of situation than I've ever faced, and I don't want it to change.

I leave the bathroom and head back to the kitchen so I can make him some food. Getting to watch him discover the world for the first time through his meals is something that I don't think is going to go anywhere. He just has such a joy for life, and I don't want to see it taken from him.

Which is a bit of a problem when he's cursed and could end up back in his teapot at any moment.

I push the thought aside. Even if he does end up in the teapot again, I'll do everything I can to hunt it down and free him, even if it takes me fifty years. Though I hope it won't. I don't want to lose any time with him.

I chop an onion and start browning it in the pan, intending to make a Spanish dish Mum taught me to make in my teens. It's not something he's had yet, but I think he'll like it. The only food he hasn't seemed much of a fan of so far is Moroccan itself, though I suspect that's because it's not the food he remembers from his life there. Maybe I need to look up some historical websites to see if there's any indication of what I can do to recreate it for him.

I let out a loud sigh and continue cooking. I know I shouldn't let myself get too lost in our relationship, especially when I'm not even fully sure that this is one. But it's also too late.

The bathroom door creaks open and I sense Azíl making his way over to me. He wraps his arms around my waist and leans his chin against my shoulder. "It smells good."

"So do you," I respond.

"I am glad you think so. These are all things you bought."

"Well, yes. But if you don't like them, we can get something different," I respond. "We can go out later and pick some up?"

"Hmm."

I frown, sensing the hesitation in his voice. "You don't want to?"

"It is not that."

"Then what is it?"

I pull the pan off the stove and divide the food into two bowls. I hand one to him, brushing my fingers against his as I take it.

"It is nothing," he says as he retreats to the sofa.

"It obviously isn't." I head over to join him along with my plate of steaming food.

He glances away, but I can tell from the expression on his face that he's going to tell me what's on his mind if I give him the time to formulate his thoughts properly.

"It is just that I never pay for anything," he says.

"That isn't true."

"Is it not? When we go out for food, you are the one who pays. Now that I need clothes and things for the shower, you are getting those too. And Sabine mentioned something about the mortgage on the coffee shop and flat, what is that?"

I let out a loud sigh, almost cursing my best friend for her lack of thought in bringing that up. "I'd be paying the same amount off the mortgage even if you weren't here," I point out.

"I do not know what it is."

"Oh, well when I bought the coffee shop, I didn't have enough money, so I borrowed some from the bank. I pay back a bit of that every month."

"Ah. So the bank controls the money? And gives you the card that you use to pay for things?"

"Yes." I know it's more complicated than that, but for now, I'll leave it at that. I can find him some beginner lessons on finances later.

"And I can get one of the cards?"

I nod. "If we open a bank account for you, then yes."

"But it will not have money in it."

"I'm paying you for your shifts in the coffee shop," I point out. "I've just been paying you in food, but there's plenty left that I can put in an account for you when you have one." The only reason I haven't is because he doesn't have the right paperwork to open one.

"I would like that."

"Okay, I'll make an appointment," I promise.

"Thank you." He takes a bite of his food.

"What made you ask today?" It's not that I mind, but I'm always curious about what catches his attention.

"The cupids were talking about the rules of dating."

I repress a groan. I really wish he wouldn't try and learn about modern dating from a show that's most likely staged. I'm sure some of it is real, particularly with the cupids reputation as matchmakers on the line, but a lot will be played up for drama. "What did they say?"

"That the man should pay for the date."

I don't stop the sigh from escaping me. "That's an antiquated rule."

"Sabine would say that I am antiquated," he counters.

"I'm sure she would," I mutter, cursing my best friend inwardly. She knows he's susceptible to these kinds of things, she should be doing a better job of minding her words around him. "But it's still true. There's no need for a man to be paying for a date. Besides, what happens when there isn't a man on the date? Or there are two? Who pays then?"

He frowns as he considers my question. "The cupids didn't say."

"What do you think?" I ask more curiously.

"I suppose the people on the date would discuss the options up front to decide who should pay," he responds.

"Then that is what should be done here too."

He nods. "That does make sense. It does seem like the fairest solution."

"It does." I'm glad he seems satisfied with the answer. I know it can't be easy for him to have to get used to modern ideals when he's grown up with something so different, but he seems eager to learn, even if I some-times forget that he doesn't know things that come naturally to me.

"In which case, I would like to take you on a date where I pay," he responds.

I smile affectionately at him. "Then we can do that."

"You do not argue?" He frowns, as if he expected me to disagree with his plan.

"No. I don't believe you have to pay, but that doesn't mean you can't. And I can tell that this is important to you." I reach out and touch his hand. "That makes it important to me."

He beams widely. "I look forward to our date, Willow."

"Me too." Even if we don't have a proper name for what's going on between us, it's clear that he believes it's as important as I do. And that's enough for now.

Chapter 2

I set the takeaway cup down in front of my current customer with a bright smile. "Thank you for coming to Cauldron Coffee Shop," I say brightly.

They take it and murmur a thanks before heading out of the door, leaving the shop surprisingly empty. I know it won't last too long, but it's nice to have a respite every once in a while.

"I am done with the stockroom," Azíl says, making his way back behind the counter. "I believe you need more of the sugar cubes."

"Because we've run out, or because

you've tried eating them again?" I ask with a raised eyebrow.

"I did not *try* to eat them, I ate one successfully."

I roll my eyes, but only with good-natured intent. "Okay, did you successfully eat them all again?" I ask instead.

"I did not."

The bell above the door rings before I can ask him any further questions. I turn to take the customer's order only to realise it's Sabine.

I grab an iced coffee cup, already knowing what she's going to order. "You look smart," I say to her as I start to make her drink.

"I have a second interview for the dig I was telling you about," she says.

"The one Sawyer got you?"

She nods. "Though it seems like I'm going to have a few to choose from. I hate it when that happens, it means I have to pick where to go."

"Is having options not good?" Azíl asks, far more at ease with her than he was before.

"It is and it isn't," she responds with a shrug. "I like being able to choose what I spend my time on, but I also worry about missing out on the things the other digs have to offer."

"Ah, that is FOMO, is it not?"

Both Sabine and I stare at him in response to the acronym. I don't think I've ever heard him use one before.

"Did I not use that right?" he asks, looking between the two of us.

"You did," I respond, setting the iced coffee down in front of Sabine. "But I don't think I've ever heard you say something as modern as FOMO. It was weird."

Sabine nods. "It's like seeing slang on ancient monuments."

"Slang," he repeats, saying the word slowly as if trying to get used to it. "I believe we have slang in our language too."

"I know," Sabine responds. "Or I assumed as much. I'm yet to encounter an ancient language that doesn't have it. But when I see it there's always a moment where I don't believe it's real."

Azíl chuckles. "Perhaps one day you will need my assistance with the slang of my people."

"If I do, I will pay you handsomely as a language expert," she promises.

A wide smile spreads over his face. "You will have to pay it into my bank account." He glances at me to check he's said that right.

I smile at him in return.

"You're getting a bank account?" Sabine asks.

"Willow is helping me."

I nod to my best friend. "He's human now, remember?"

"Mmm, yes. That's a good point. How is human life treating you?"

"Better than being cursed to live in a teapot." His response is surprisingly quick. "But I must admit that it is harder to be without my magic than I expected."

My heart aches for him. I wish I

could do something to make it easier for him, but it seems that disconnecting him with the teapot hasn't resulted in the return of the innate powers he was born with.

I'm not sure how he's managing to function. I may not be as magic reliant as some witches, but I can't even imagine how little time it would take me to grow impatient with the world if I couldn't do a spell here or there.

"Hopefully that will change once your curse is broken," Sabine says.

"I believe it will," Azíl says. "Though if my magic never returns, it is a small price to pay for my freedom."

"That won't happen," I assure him.

"You don't know that," Sabine says carefully. "Curses can have strange side effects and Azíl has been under one for a very long time, we don't know what's going to happen when we manage to break the curse." She takes a drink.

I bite my bottom lip, hating that she's right but knowing she is. I don't want Azíl to lose anything, even though it's far too late for that when he hasn't had his freedom for three thousand years.

Azíl reaches out to me and takes my hand in his, giving it a squeeze. He doesn't say anything, but I know what he's trying to tell me all the same. I appreciate the gesture, but it does nothing to alleviate my guilt, even if I know it isn't mine to carry. I'm not the one who did this to him.

"We'll find a solution," I say. "Even if we have to go on a trek across Morocco to find it." My voice cracks, but I manage to hold it together.

"I don't think it will come to that," Sabine counters. "Though I've heard it's a lovely holiday destination, perhaps you should go. Will you be getting Azíl a passport?"

I nod. "I've set up the appointments at the Bureau for Witch and Warlock Affairs already."

"A passport?" Azíl echoes.

Right, he's never needed one before.

"It's what lets you travel between countries." Sabine pulls hers out of her bag and hands it to him.

I raise an eyebrow. "And you just happen to be carrying yours? Are you expecting Sawyer to whisk you off on an unexpected getaway?"

Sabine lets out an amused chuckle. "He knows that isn't wise. But no, I need it for the interview."

Azíl studies it in detail. "It says you are a necromancer on it, but you do not like people knowing that," he says.

My best friend lets out a hum of agreement. "You have to have your species listed."

"Will mine say human or warlock?" he asks.

"Warlock," I say firmly.

Sabine nods in agreement. "That's what you were born, and what your children would be born as."

"Children," he repeats.

"Hypothetical children." She flashes me an apologetic look. "*If* you had children, they would be warlocks, so long as you had them with a witch, anyway."

"I do not understand."

Sabine's expression begs me to help her.

I shrug. "You're the one who brought up supernatural genetics."

She lets out a loud sigh. "Yep, that's on me. I don't imagine your clan knew much about other supernatural types?" She takes a sip of her iced coffee.

"We knew that they existed, and that they had lives we did not understand, but I believe I have met more supernaturals in the few months I have been here, than I did in thirty years."

"As expected," Sabine says. "Well, anyone can marry anyone..."

"But they do not need to," Azíl supplies. "Willow taught me that."

"Did she?" Sabine raises an eyebrow at me, but I busy myself with wiping up an invisible coffee spill so I don't have to look at her.

"She said that it is a personal choice who someone marries and if they marry. And that some things that would have been saved for marriage in my clan do not require such a ceremony now."

Sabine lets out a soft snort. "I think I just learned more about your love life than I wanted to," she mutters.

I roll my eyes. "The conversation was all hypothetical." Though what happened after it was not.

"Mmhmm. Anyway, if a witch and a warlock have a child together, it will be a witch or warlock, but if a witch and a vampire have a child, it will be a vampire because their DNA is stronger. I don't know the exact ins and outs of it, but there's a hierarchy of DNA. It's why there aren't dozens of hybrids running around. Though there are a few combinations where that's still possible."

Azíl frowns. "But witches and warlocks are also different species."

Sabine and I share a confused glance.

"No, we're the same species," I say slowly.

"This must have changed," he says. "There were at least warlocks, witches, mages, and sorcerers known to my clan, there may have been more. Each of them could do something different and had different magic."

Excitement dances in Sabine's eyes. "Are you serious?"

He frowns. "Why would I not be?"

"Do you realise what this means?" She is almost bouncing up and down on the balls of her feet.

"Clearly not," I respond.

She's almost bursting at the seams, which at least means that she's going to tell us and not just keep us in the dark. "People have speculated about the combining of the magic wielder lines for years. There are papers on it, but no one has ever been able to prove that they were completely separate species."

"Right, I think I read an article on that a while back, I just thought it was a theory," I admit. And not one that makes much difference to my life. If it's true, then it doesn't change anything about my abilities. If it isn't, then there's still no change.

"It's exciting," Sabine assures me. "It could mean amazing things for my career if I'm the one who can prove this is true. And with Azíl's help, I could be."

"Perhaps, but you're forgetting that he can't be carbon dated like one of your fossils."

"Fossils aren't really my speciality," she counters.

"That's not my point, Sabby," I respond. "In order for anything Azíl says to be taken as fact, he needs to be known as a three-thousand-year-old warlock, and that's just not provable. Is it?" I look between the two of them, not knowing which of them is going to have an answer for me.

"I do not believe so," Azíl responds.

Sabine lets out a loud sigh. "I know, I know. But he can guide me to the right places to find the proof I need. Or he can help me decipher things that I find. I mean, if you're interested in that, Azíl?"

"It does sound intriguing," he responds.

I cross my arms and give them both a stern look. "You're both forgetting that we have bigger problems to deal with right now than the genetic history of witches and warlocks," I say. "Like breaking curses and getting to job interviews."

Sabine's eyes widen. "Right, I should get going. Thanks for the coffee, I'll be back later."

"You'd better be, I have the new coffee shot for you to try arriving tomorrow."

She nods and starts to head for the door, waving goodbye to us as she does.

I let out a loud sigh. I should have known that Sabine wasn't going to just let me have my three-thousand-year-old boyfriend in peace. She'll need all the information she can get out of him in order to find out more about the ancient world.

At least she's stopped disapproving of the situation. I can live with the rest of it if that is the case.

Chapter 3

The building which houses the Bureau for Witch and Warlock Affairs is a lot greyer and drabber than I expect it to be, which is how I realise I've never actually been here before.

I reach out and take Azíl's hand in mine, giving it a squeeze. "We don't have to do this if you don't want to," I assure him. "They're going to ask a lot of questions."

He takes a shaky breath. "I am concerned about if this is the right decision," he responds. "But I am starting to believe that it will be possible to break my curse, and if that is true, then I believe that I will need to do this anyway."

I give him a small smile that I hope is reassuring. I *want* him to believe that it's going to be possible to break his curse. There's still a long way to go to make that possible, especially when Mona and Daphne haven't made any progress in actually deciphering any of the secrets of the teapot yet, but that doesn't mean we have to pause our lives.

"Let's get this over with," I say. "Then we can go back to the coffee shop and unpack the box of cakes my cousins sent over."

"What have they sent?" he asks.

"A little of everything if Hazel is to be believed." And she generally is. Despite being the youngest of the four of them, she's often the one who can be relied on the most when it comes to this kind of thing.

"I look forward to discovering something new."

I smile at him, certain he's telling the truth.

I try to ignore the nerves fluttering away inside me as we enter the building. It looks no different from any other official offices I've been in, but somehow it feels different. Maybe I'm worried they're going to tell me I've done something wrong by accidentally freeing Azíl. Or by not helping him earlier.

Or perhaps my nerves are more to do with the fact that we're about to tell someone the entire story of how Azíl even came to be here in the first place.

"Good morning, how can I help you?" the woman behind the desk asks.

"We have an appointment with the cursed beings department?" I say, hoping that's the right one.

"Head down the corridor and it's third on the right," she says. "Ask for Wilfred."

"Right, okay, thanks;." Somehow, I didn't expect it to be that easy. Is this a sign that it's all going to be, or that things are about to get really difficult?

I try not to think about it too much and follow her instructions.

Azíl follows behind me, his nervousness coming off him in waves. As hard as this is going to be for me, it's going to be so much worse for him. He's never had to come anywhere like this. When he was last free, he'll have known his clan members for his entire life. Now I'm bringing him to all kinds of strange places and doing things that didn't even have words when he's from.

I try to give him a reassuring smile, which he responds to in kind. It wrinkles up the corners of his eyes, only reminding me of the kindness that is always lingering just beneath the surface.

Sometimes, it's hard to believe he's this good when he's been through so much, and all it does is make me more determined to break the cycle and ensure that he's freed. He may not want to stay at the coffee shop with me once he is, but that's a risk I'm willing to take for his freedom.

"This should be it," I say when we approach the right door. "Are you ready?"

"I am not. But that does not mean we should not do this."

I know he's right, but that barely keeps me from running away and not looking back. Instead, I raise my fist and knock twice.

"Come in," a man calls.

I take a deep breath and step into the room.

The office is less cluttered than I expect, with a wide window and an almost empty desk with a middle-aged man sitting behind it.

"Hi, I'm Willow Reid, we have an appointment."

"Ah, yes I've been expecting you, why don't you have a seat Ms Reid." He gestures to the chairs opposite him.

I do as he asks, while Azíl follows behind me, clearly as uncomfortable as I am, but not wanting to say anything.

The plaque on his desk confirms he's the person we've been sent to, and nothing about him seems to stand out, from his slightly thinning hair to his run-of-the-mill suit. It isn't until I catch sight of the pin on his lapel that I find myself stopping and scrutinising him more. It's vaguely familiar, a circle with a single line through it, but I can't put my finger on where I've seen it before.

"Let's get right to it, shall we," Wilfred says. "I believe you're here about a cursed being?"

"Yes," I respond.

"Have you kept good records of where you think this being resides so we can investigate?"

"Ah, erm, you seem to have gotten the wrong idea," I say.

He raises an eyebrow. "How so?"

"We're not here to report a cursed being, we're here to register a formerly cursed one." I reach out and take Azíl's hand in mine, giving it a squeeze.

"Ah, then we're going to need some other forms. If you'll give me a moment." He gets to his feet and bustles out of the room, leaving the two of us alone.

"Do you think this will be a problem?" Azíl asks.

I shake my head. "It should be fine." I hope. The department is supposed to help with this kind of thing, and Azíl is a warlock, that should help. "It's going to be okay."

He chuckles deeply. "You sound like you are trying to convince yourself."

I let out a loud sigh. "I think I am."

Wilfred reenters the room before we can continue our conversation and takes a seat behind his desk. "Right, so, we're registering a formerly cursed being," he says.

"Yes," I respond. Though technically, it isn't quite the truth. Azíl is still cursed, he's just not attached to his teapot anymore.

"I will assume that it is you?" Wilfred asks Azíl.

"It is."

He nods. "And you are a warlock?"

"I am."

"Very well. What is your date of birth?"

Azíl's eyes widen. "I am not sure."

The man opposite us raises an eyebrow. "How can you not be sure?"

"I was born a long time ago," Azíl responds. "We measured time differently."

Wilfred lets out a loud sigh, making me dislike him even more. "Let's try a different question. What is your name?"

"Azíl."

"And your surname?"

"I do not have one."

Wilfred's frustration is clear on his face. "Then you will have to be Azíl Smith until you decide on one." He writes it down on his form.

I wrinkle my nose. It's not a name that suits Azíl, though I know it's one of those things that will have to do until he can come up with the right name.

"How long were you cursed?" Wilfred asks.

"I believe it was around three thousand years," Azíl responds.

"And your place of cursing?"

"Morocco."

"Morocco?" He sits up, seeming a little more interested than before. He touches the pin at his lapel, drawing my attention back to it.

Something about the situation makes me feel uneasy.

"I believe that is what you call it now," Azíl says. I can tell from the way he's speaking that he's nervous about the situation. I wish I could make it easier for him. It must be difficult to talk so openly about this when it's been a secret for as long as it has.

"Do you know whereabouts in Morocco?" Wilfred asks eagerly.

"I do not know the modern name."

"Understandable, understandable," he mutters with a nod of his head. "And how were you cursed? Do you know who was responsible?"

"No."

I try not to respond to his lie, not wanting to give Azíl away.

"I was cursed to live in a small space and was only freed recently."

Wilfred touches his pin again, and it suddenly hits me where I've seen it before. Aisha was wearing a pin like that when she tried to use blood magic on me, and I saw it later in one of the books Sabine gave us.

An uneasy feeling settles within me, but I push it away. I don't know what the pin means, it could be completely unrelated to the entire situation, and I certainly don't know enough about it to make any judgments on the situation.

"Are you also applying for any assistance or a place to live? We have programs that will help with that?"

"I wish to remain with Willow," he says firmly, looking at me for reassurance.

Wilfred lets out a disappointed sigh. Or maybe I'm imagining it. I feel like I'm getting myself worked up for nothing right now. "I'll start the process of creating the necessary records, but you will need to fill in these." He pushes a huge stack of forms in our direction. "There are all the necessary forms here for you to sponsor Azíl," he says to me.

"Thank you." I pull them over and slip them into my bag.

"I will also email you with another appointment for us to go through everything. After that, we should be able to get Mr Smith everything he needs in order to have an official identity. Only if your forms are all filled in, naturally."

"We'll make sure everything is done perfectly," I assure him, already getting to my feet. "Thank you for your help."

Azíl echoes my goodbye, and I hurry from the building, hoping I can leave my sense of unease behind me as I do.

Chapter 4

I finish cleaning the coffee machine and head back around to the customer side of the shop to find a frustrated-looking Azíl staring at the form in front of him.

"Can I help?" I ask, sitting down opposite him.

"I do not understand half of the questions," he admits. "How am I supposed to fill out the form?"

"Let me have a look?" I hold out my hand.

He gives it to me, relief flashing through his eyes as I start to look down the questions.

"This is ridiculous," I mutter. "How are you supposed to put in a phone number when you can't get one?"

"So it is not something I am missing?"

"No. But we can put mine down." I take the pen and start filling in the contact details with my own. I'm sure I'll have to repeat it all when I get to the forms that allow me to sponsor Azíl as living here, but it's worth it.

"I still do not know what to put for the surname question. Azíl Smith does not feel right."

I chuckle. "No, it does not."

"Could I use yours?"

I blink a few times. "I mean, you can if you want."

"Is that not a normal thing to ask? You seem surprised."

"Well, people normally only share a surname if they're related..."

"We do not want that." He flashes me a cheeky grin.

I chuckle. "I don't think anyone's

going to think that. We don't look related."

"True. You are very pale."

A small snort escapes me. "That's because I stay inside all the time. But what I was going to say was that people who share surnames are either related or married. And if it's the latter, it's normally the woman who takes the man's name."

He frowns. "That does not seem in line with many of the modern opinions you have told me about."

"I suppose it isn't, but that is the way it is."

"Very well, I will come up with a surname for myself."

"Did your clan have a name?" I ask.

"Yes."

"But you probably don't want to use that."

"No. Their betrayal is not something I wish to carry with me. Nor would they wish me to. In cursing me, they banished me from my clan."

"Not a good choice then. Did your people have a name for yourselves collectively? Like all the clans?"

"I do not know what you mean."

"Oh, well like I'm British because I come from the UK, but my family name is Reid."

"Ah, I see. We called ourselves Amazigh."

"What does it mean?"

I can see him trying to work through the translation in his head until a small smile curls at his lips. "Free men."

"Then I think it's perfect."

"Azíl Amazigh," he says. "I like it. Will you put it on the form for me?"

"Of course." I write it down. "We're going to have to work out some answers for date and place of birth though."

"I was born in a tent."

"I don't think that's what they mean. But I suppose *unknown* is a good answer to make sure there isn't too much information about you in the file.

The warlocks who want to replace your curse are still out there, we can't be too careful," I say.

"That is true."

"I worry about it," I admit quietly. "I don't want them to find you before we can break your curse."

"I do not particularly want them to find me once we have broken it either," he points out.

"I know. But once we've done that, it'll be easier for us to protect you."

He reaches over and takes my hand in his. "I am sorry for bringing so many problems into your life." His accent grows slightly thicker through his emotions.

"Never be sorry for coming here," I respond with as much earnestness as I can. "I am glad Sabine found your teapot, and that she sent you here."

"I will try not to be."

"*Meow.*"

The sudden interruption makes me jump and I turn to find Spooky with her head cocked to the side studying me and her tail flicking from side to side.

"It would appear that Spooky agrees with you," he says.

I chuckle. "I've no doubt she does. Half of this is her fault," I remind him.

"That is true. I owe you my freedom, Miss Spooky." He takes off an imaginary hat and does a little bow towards her.

A small laugh escapes me. "Thank you, Spooky," I echo.

"Meow."

"Do you know what that means?" I ask Azíl.

He shrugs. "The ability to decipher her meaning seems to have been a skill related to the teapot. I do not have it any longer."

"Oh." I can't help but feel disappointed by that. I like it when he tells me that Spooky feels affection towards me.

As if she can sense my thoughts, Spooky starts making her way towards me. I can't take my eyes off her and worry begins to fill me as I realise she's limping.

I set my pen down on the table and crouch down on the floor next to the cat. "Are you okay?" I ask her. "Are you hurt?"

Slowly, I reach out to pet her head, surprised that she lets me.

She sits down again, holding her front left paw gingerly above the floor and not putting any weight on it.

"What has happened?" Azíl asks.

"I don't know. She seems to have hurt herself. Can I look?" I ask the cat, reaching out for her paw.

She hisses loudly, making it clear that I'm not to go anywhere near it.

"Okay, but you can't walk around on that," I remind her. I sit back on my heels and look at Azíl. "I think we're going to have to take her to the vet."

Spooky lets out another loud hiss.

"Is there one open at this time?"

I nod. "They always stay open past nightfall for the vampires."

"Ah, yes. I forgot. We did not have many of those where I am from."

"I imagine there's too much daylight for them," I agree. "It must suck to not be able to go out in the sun."

"I do not think that is the only thing about vampires that sucks," he jokes.

I raise an eyebrow. "Did you learn that one from *Fang Me?*"

"I did," he responds with pride.

I shake my head in amusement. "I thought you weren't going to watch that to try and learn about the modern world anymore?"

"I am not watching it to learn, but I can not seem to stop watching."

Amusement fills me. "You're addicted to the show."

"I do not know what that means."

"It doesn't matter," I promise. "Will you get me one of the cardboard boxes from behind the counter and a cushion?" Without a pet carrier, that's going to have to do for getting Spooky to the vet.

He nods and disappears to get what I've asked.

"I know you're not going to be a big fan of this," I say to the cat. "But if you're hurt, then we need to get you help." Even if it means I'm probably going to have to face the reality that she belongs to someone else.

As much as I don't want that, I also know that Spooky's health is more important than my denial.

Azíl returns with the box and sets it down next to us. To my surprise, Spooky gets up and starts to investigate it. Maybe this is going to be easier than I thought.

Chapter 5

I pace back and forth in the vet's waiting room, trying not to worry too much about the cat we've handed over.

"Willow, you should sit down," Azíl says.

"I can't."

He nods.

Despite my protest, I drop into the chair next to him with a loud sigh. "I'm just worried about what the vet will say."

"Because you are worried about Spooky?"

"Partly."

"Ah, because you are worried

about your heart," he says. "You think the vet will tell you that Spooky can not be yours."

Tears spring to my eyes, and I wipe them away quickly. "I know it's silly of me. She's never been my cat. And it's not like I'm even a cat person, I had a hamster growing up."

"I do not know what that is."

"I'll show you a picture later," I promise. "I've never had a cat, and I didn't think I wanted one, but the idea of not having Spooky around..."

"That is because you do not want *a* cat, you want Spooky. It is a natural thing."

"You think?"

He nods. "Many moons ago, I had a fear of horses."

"Horses?"

"Mmhmm."

"I thought you lived in a clan that moved around a lot?"

"I did," he confirms.

"Ah, I can see how a fear of horses could be a problem."

"It was. A foal was born, he was brown, with a white patch over his eye. Like this." He traces an oval around his eye to demonstrate.

"Was that unusual?"

"It was considered bad luck," he admits. "And they said that no one would be interested in riding the horse once they were grown."

"Because he had a white patch over his eye?" I can't help the surprised confusion entering my voice.

"I agree that it is a strange reason. I was too young to understand that the elders believed the horse to be unsuitable, but I realised no one liked him. I went to sit with him a few times."

"Even though you were scared of horses?" I ask.

Azíl nods. "I worried that he was lonely. Over time, I realised that I was no longer scared of horses, though I did not like the others the way I liked him."

"What happened?" I think I know, but the way Azíl grew up and the culture he lived in are so different from the one I'm used to that I don't want to make assumptions based on that.

"I finally started to learn to ride," he says. "I was very sad when he died."

I reach out and put my hand over his. "I'm sorry. Did he have a name?"

"White patch."

I frown. "White patch?"

"It does not sound as good in English," he admits.

"Will you say it in your language?"

He repeats the name in what I assume is his native tongue, but with very little knowledge of what the Berber people used to speak, I can't tell.

"It's a beautiful name," I say, meaning the words. "And I like your voice when you're speaking in your language."

He chuckles and says something different.

"What does that mean?" I ask.

"I told you that you are more beautiful than a hundred rising moons," he responds.

I look away, a blush rushing to my cheeks. "Thank you."

He's about to respond when the vet steps back into the room and clears his throat. "Ms Reid, do you have a moment?"

I nod and get to my feet.

"I've done an examination of the cat and located the injury to her paw," the vet says.

I let out a sigh of relief. "So it's just an external injury? Nothing more serious?"

"She is in good health," he assures me. "However..."

I close my eyes, already knowing what he's going to say. "You found a chip."

"I did."

"Thank you for checking," I say, fighting back more of the tears that had threatened earlier.

"You did the right thing bringing her here," the vet says. "But as I'm sure you are aware, I can't let you leave with her."

"I understand. Can I at least say goodbye to her?"

"You'll have to be supervised while you do," he responds.

"I understand." And I do. I know I'm not about to steal Spooky, but he doesn't know me at all. For all he knows, I've given him a false name.

"Very well, come with me." He leads me into the examination room where Spooky is sitting on a padded bench with her paw wrapped in a bandage.

Azíl follows behind silently.

"Hey, Spooky," I say as I reach out and stroke the cat's head.

She purrs and pushes it against my hand, only causing a sob to explode from me.

Azíl places a hand on my lower back and rubs it in a show of silent support. I appreciate it more than I can tell him right now. I shouldn't be as bothered by this as I am. I've always known that Spooky isn't my cat. That fact isn't a surprise to me.

"You've been great company," I say to her. "And you brought something truly special into my life." I almost look at Azíl.

"Meow?" She looks up at me with such confusion in her eyes that I can't take it.

"Goodbye, Spooky." I turn away, knowing that I can't say anything else without completely breaking apart. "Thank you," I say to the vet as we pass.

My heart aches as we leave, hating every moment of the situation even though I've known it's coming for a while.

I hurry out of the clinic, not stopping to take a breath until I'm outside and in the fresh air.

Azíl tugs me into his arms and I go willingly, accepting the comfort he's giving me.

"She will probably visit again," he says.

I sniff and wipe my eyes, not leaving his embrace. "I know, but it won't be the same."

"You do not know that. Your bond with Spooky is not something that can be undone just because she lives somewhere else. You always knew that was the case. The only thing that has changed is that you know for certain that she has an owner."

"You're right." I step back and dry my eyes. There's no doubt in my mind that what he's saying is true, the thing I don't know is how I'm going to feel when Spooky is back at the coffee shop being her normal self.

At least there are plenty of other things going on for me to distract myself with. I don't have to focus on this. Besides, like Azíl says, it may not feel any different once things return to normal and Spooky is still in my life.

I look in his direction. If this is how bad I feel about realising that Spooky can't stay with me, then what's going to happen if he ends up cursed and back in his teapot for the next hundred years? I've never been the kind of person who let relationships control my life, but this feels different. Maybe because Azíl has so quickly become a part of it.

Whatever the reasons, while I'm sure I'd survive, I don't think I'd ever be the same again if I lost him to his curse.

Which only makes me more determined than ever to make sure that doesn't happen.

Chapter 6

Wilfred's office in the Bureau for Witch and Warlock Affairs looks exactly the same as last time, which I suppose is to be expected considering the fact that it's barely been a week since we were last here.

The stack of forms we've meticulously filled in and checked three times sits on the desk in front of Wilfred while he flips through them, nodding and occasionally typing something into his computer.

No matter how benign he seems to be acting, my attention keeps straying back to the pin at his lapel and wondering about what it means. It can't be a coincidence that it's the same one Aisha was wearing while she was at the coffee shop, can it?

I need to ask Sabine if she knows more about it, but I haven't had a chance yet.

"I see there is some information missing on the location of cursing," Wilfred says, looking straight at Azíl. "Is that something you can fill in for us, Mr Amazigh?"

"I do not know the place," he says.

"I'm sure there must be something you can remember about it," Wilfred responds. "A local town name?"

"There was no local town to my knowledge," Azíl responds. "It was in the middle of the wilderness."

"Hmm." He writes something down. "Do you know what the place is called now?"

"I apologise, but I do not know modern-day Morocco, I have never been."

I reach out and take Azíl's hand, sensing how difficult he's finding this.

"What about the time of cursing, do you know that?"

"It was at night, but I was asleep and do not know time better than that."

"Very well. This is going to make things difficult unless you have more information about your curse."

"I have included everything I remember on the forms as instructed," Azíl says. "It is a long time ago, and I was preoccupied at the time of my cursing."

Wilfred purses his lips, clearly unhappy with Azíl's answer despite the fact it should be obvious that is the case.

"You have also left birthplace blank save for writing Morocco," the man prompts.

"I do not have more information to add."

"Mr Amazigh, I realise this may be a difficult process for you, but without as much information as possible, we are going to struggle to get you the paperwork you need in order to register properly," Wilfred says sternly.

"He's telling you everything he knows," I put in. "It's been three thousand years, I'm not sure about you, but I don't remember important things from three years ago, never mind that long."

"I see your point, Ms Reid, but I hope you understand that this kind of thing can cause delays that I'm not sure either you or Mr Amazigh want."

"Isn't there something that can be done?" I prompt. "This can't be the first time you're dealing with a cursed being from thousands of years ago."

"It may surprise you to know that we're not the busiest of departments, Ms Reid."

"Then I'm sure you'll agree that it's good to have a challenge such as the one we're posing," I respond, crossing my arms and leaning back in my chair.

An amused expression flits over Azíl's face, but he covers it quickly.

Wilfred eyes me suspiciously, as if wondering whether I'm here because I want to register Azíl, or because I'm doing some kind of audit on him and how well he does his job. I suppose it isn't bad for me if he believes the latter. It takes suspicion away from Azíl and the truth behind where he came from, and will make sure everything gets processed faster. I don't mind either of those outcomes given the circumstances.

Especially with the uneasy feeling that keeps settling within me every time Wilfred asks another question. I know it's his job to make sure everything runs smoothly, but it almost feels like there's another motivation behind the way he's asking, but I can't put my finger on what it is.

Other than the pin he's wearing, but that could mean nothing.

Wilfred types into his computer and then nods sharply. "It seems as if you are correct, Ms Reid. There are allowances for situations such as this. I will make sure to fill in that part of the form for you."

"Thank you," I respond, feeling at least a little satisfied about that.

He taps a few keys and the printer begins to whirr. "You'll need to sign this," Wilfred says, grabbing it from the printer and handing it to Azíl. "And then we'll need to take a photo for your passport."

"Does that not have to be done through the passport office?" I ask, worried about why he might want a picture of Azíl. I push the thought aside. Even if it was for a nefarious reason, which seems unlikely, the people who are trying to curse Azíl don't know what he looks like. They would have to already know to look for his file in order to match the two of them up.

"Not in cases like this. We work with them in order to fulfil the needs of formerly cursed beings," Wilfred says.

"Though I have noticed a lack of detail about the curse breaking."

Azíl and I exchange a look.

"We're not exactly clear on that ourselves," I lie. "There was some restorative magic, and then Azíl was free. Neither of us were aware of what happened."

"That is not uncommon, though it was fortunate that the spell you used was the countercurse," Wilfred says, eyeing us suspiciously.

"It was." I smile, hoping it appears to be genuinely reassuring.

"Where did this occur?"

"Cauldron Coffee Shop. The address is on the forms as Azíl's current residence."

Wilfred raises an eyebrow but doesn't say anything. It still worries me to be giving him all of this information, but I know that he needs it in order to do his job.

Even so, it leaves Azíl vulnerable, and I don't like it.

"All right, follow me and we'll get your picture taken," Wilfred says.

Azíl gives my hand a reassuring squeeze and gets up to follow him.

Waiting is going to be excruciating, but I don't think they're going to be gone long enough for me to snoop around Wilfred's office, which is a shame as I feel it might alleviate some of my concerns.

This is nothing more than run-of-the-mill-bureaucracy, and I need to remember that before I drive myself crazy with the possibilities.

Chapter 7

I set the teapot and two tea glasses down in the middle of the table and sit down opposite Azíl. I pour us both a cup, making sure to add a generous drizzle of honey to Azíl's. I need to take him to a farmer's market so he can pick out his favourite type of honey, but there hasn't been time yet.

"You are having mint tea with me?" he asks as he picks up his glass and blows across the top of it.

I nod. "My stomach has been in knots ever since our meeting with Wilfred," I admit. "I thought this might help. Mint tea is supposed to do that."

"It has many good qualities," he agrees. "What is bothering you about the meeting?" he asks.

"I don't know. It's just a feeling. You know?"

"I do not think my alarm system is something we should be relying on," he jokes.

I chuckle. "Perhaps not. Though I imagine the people who cursed you were prepared for the situation given how powerful you are." I frown. "Or are you?"

"For my time, I was a talented warlock, yes. For your time, I am not sure. It is hard to tell. There are many more things that magic seems to be able to do in your times, but I do not know if they are stronger or weaker than in my own."

"That's fair. Hopefully, we'll find out when you get your magic back."

"That may not happen, Willow."

"It will," I say firmly.

"It does not matter if it does. I have been thinking, and if we are not able to break my curse but I can continue living this way, then that is something I could come to terms with."

"You could?"

He nods. "I am mortal again. I feel hunger and pain, that is good."

"That's an odd combination to be pleased about," I mutter.

"That is not true. Before I came here, I felt good emotions with the others who have accidentally allowed me out of my teapot. I felt curiosity and I knew learning."

"And when I did the same?" My voice comes out surprisingly small, as if I'm worried about what he's going to say.

He sets down his glass of tea and reaches over, taking my hand in his. "I have felt many things since you let me out of the teapot."

"Including hunger and pain, apparently."

He chuckles. "And many good things. I have felt friendship, and hope."

"Those are both good."

"And I also feel something I haven't before, I..."

The door opens and I curse myself for not having locked it. Normally the closed sign does the trick at this time in the evening.

"It's just me," Sabine says in a sing-song voice.

For a moment, I consider telling her to go away, especially with the earnestness in Azíl's voice and the direction of the conversation. I think I know what he was going to say, and now I'll have to wait.

She heads over to us and sits down on one of the spare seats. "How did the meeting at the Bureau go?" she asks.

"Fine, I think," I respond. "They asked a lot of questions."

"What about?"

"Where Azíl is from and the details about his curse."

"They may have needed that information," Sabine says in a matter-of-fact tone.

I let out a loud sigh. "I know, I know. It was just a feeling."

"Ah, one of those. Well you shouldn't ignore a witch's intuition, you know that. How did you feel?" she asks Azíl.

He shrugs. "It is all so strange to me still that it did not register as particularly odd, other than the way Willow responded."

"Sorry," I mutter.

"There is no need to be. You should not dismiss your feelings. I trust them." He gives me a reassuring smile to go along with his words.

"Where *are* you from?" Sabine asks.

"I do not think that I can say without a map."

"I have one," she says excitedly, pulling a map out of her bag.

"You just happen to be carrying around a map of Morocco?" I ask.

She chuckles. "Considering my friend's boyfriend is an ancient warlock from there, I thought it might be appropriate."

I glance at Azíl to see how he'll respond to her use of boyfriend, but it doesn't seem to have registered. We've never really talked about what our relationship is and what label we want to give it, though we probably should.

"That's not the reason," I say to my friend.

"No, it isn't," she confirms.

"Here," Azíl says, breaking through our conversation. He points to the bottom of what looks like a mountain range. "I am reasonably certain."

Sabine raises an eyebrow. "You have to be kidding me," she mutters.

"What's wrong?" I look between the two of them, feeling as if I've missed something.

Sabine takes a deep breath. "You know that interview Sawyer got for me?"

I nod.

"Well, I got the job offer today."

"That's great news, congratulations. Are you taking it, or are you going with one of your others?"

"I'm taking it," she responds. "The location is somewhere I couldn't resist."

Intrigue fills me. Knowing Sabine, that means she hasn't been there before. She always likes discovering new places. "Where is it?"

An amused smile twists at her lips and she leans forward, placing her finger on the exact spot where Azíl had moments before. "Here."

"Are you serious?" A combination of excitement and nerves fills me.

She nods. "Sawyer put me forward when he heard about the location of the dig, he thought that even if I couldn't find anything of help on the dig itself, I might be able to make some inquiries while I'm there to find something. But this is even better than that."

"Wow." I sit back in my chair, trying to process what's happening. "What are the chances?"

"Fairly high, given my profession," she quips.

I roll my eyes. "All right, fine. You're an expert on old things."

"Not as much as you are these days," she throws back.

Azíl chuckles.

I turn to glare at him, but he just shrugs. "I am not complaining."

Sabine's amusement grows. "I knew I liked you for a reason," she tells him.

"You like him because he's fascinating," I remind her. "And can tell you lots of ancient secrets."

"Yes, and now I'm going to be supervising a dig in the place he used to live. I am going to get so many more museum showings for this one."

I shake my head in amusement, pleased that she'll get to further her career *and* help at the same time.

"When do you leave?" I ask.

"Next week. There isn't much turn-around, and I still need to tell the dig in Tuscany that I won't be heading up that one. Though from what they said during that meeting, I might be able to get them to delay until I'm back," she muses.

"You're in demand."

"That's what happens when you strive to be the best in your field," she retorts.

"I wouldn't know, I own a coffee shop," I point out.

"Yes, but the *best* coffee shop in town."

"You're biassed because I charge you minimal rent."

"I think it is the best too," Azíl adds.

"And you're extra biassed," I respond, but I don't mind. I can feel the affection flowing around the room, and the hope that Sabine's dig could mean good things for Azíl's future.

Chapter 8

The postman drops a bundle of letters on my counter and disappears without saying a word. Not an uncommon occurrence when there are already customers in.

I pick them up and flick through to check if there's anything interesting, only coming to a stop when I see an envelope with Azíl's name on it.

"I think your registration stuff has arrived," I say to him, holding out the letter.

"I have correspondance?"

"You do."

Excitement enters his eyes. "This is new."

"I know."

I check around the coffee shop to make sure no one needs anything and I'm free to spend my time focusing on the man in front of me.

He tears open the envelope and pulls out a sheet of paper.

"Dear Mr Amazigh," he starts to read. "We are pleased to inform you that you are now a registered formerly cursed being residing in the United Kingdom. Your passport and National Insurance number will be on their way to you within thirty days."

"That was faster than I expected," I admit. "I thought it was going to take much longer with the way Wilfred was acting at our appointment last week."

"That is good. But what is the National Insurance number it is talking about?"

"Oh, that's for tax."

"I feel that is something else you are going to have to explain to me."

I chuckle. "How about I find you another reality TV show with it in?"

"I would rather you teach me."

I shake my head in amusement. "I will. Maybe over dinner that you can pay for yourself."

"I can do that now?"

"Not quite. We'll have to set up a bank account for you first, but we can do that tomorrow and then I can pay you your wages."

"That is what I earn by working here?"

I nod. "So you get paid based on how many hours you work. I don't know if there's anything special I need to do because you're a formerly cursed resident, but I'll check with my accountant." Which is just one more person who is going to know about Azíl. Though I suppose that's unavoidable if he's going to build a life here.

And I'm not going to begrudge him that, far from it. I want him to build a life here, and not just because it will mean that he's free from the teapot, but because it means he can build a life with me.

"I need to plan all of the things for our date," he says excitedly. "I can use your computer to find things?"

"Of course. You can even go do it now if you want, we're not too busy."

He nods. "I think I shall." He leans in and kisses my cheek. "Thank you for helping me with this, Willow."

"You're welcome." I smile at him as he hurries off to plan what I'm sure is going to be an eclectic date with far too much food involved. Not that I mind, we always have a good time.

A new customer appears, pulling me out of my thoughts and back to my present reality of making the best coffee I can.

"Thank you, have a nice day," I say to the third customer since Azíl left me in.

A stressed-looking Sabine appears through the door at the same time they leave and she hurries over to the counter as I'm already starting her drink.

"You look like you need a pick-me-up," I say.

"Mmm, I hope my dig has a dead body," she mutters under her breath.

"Don't say that too loudly."

"I know, people wouldn't like it."

"I don't have any dead bodies, but the necromancer powder I ordered arrived, want to give it a shot?" I ask after making sure no one can overhear us.

"Yeah might as well. It's not going to make me more exhausted, right?"

"I don't know why it would." I grab a sachet from under the counter and dump it into her iced coffee, making sure to stir it in thoroughly so it doesn't clump to the bottom. "Here you go."

"Thanks, Willow." She takes a sip. "Mmm, that's good. I can actually feel it feeding my magic a bit."

"It's supposed to. I don't think it works as an alternative to...you know." I wave my hand around.

"Syphoning magic off the dead?" she supplies.

"Yes, that. But it should give you, or anyone else that wants it a good pick-me-up."

"I like it. Even if you don't manage to sell it, I'll certainly be having some."

"Good."

"Where's Azíl?"

"Upstairs planning the date he's going to take me on once he has a bank account." It's impossible to ignore the affection in my voice when I say it.

"Do you know when that will be?"

"His registration came through today, so we're going to sort out a bank account tomorrow," I respond.

"Ah, did his passport come too?"

"No, not yet. Why?"

"Well, I was thinking about it, and what if I find something that means you need to come to Morocco? He's going to need a passport if you come."

"The letter said it would arrive within a month," I assure her.

"Will you be okay if you have to come over?" she asks.

"Yes, my passport has a few years left on it."

"I meant with the coffee shop."

"Oh, right." Somehow I didn't consider that might be what she meant. "If it happens, I'll talk to Clover and see if she can take over for a week or so." My cousin's done it before, and I'm sure she will again at some point in the future.

"Ah, I forgot about Clover. I mean, it might not be necessary, you'll only have to come if I find something."

"How likely do you think that will be?"

"I have no idea. I've never gone on a dig for a personal reason like this before," she admits. "But from the initial brief, it sounds like there's some potential for it to have some answers for us. The time period is right, as is the area. There are still a lot of factors, but..."

"We might be able to find something."

She nods. "That's what I'm hoping anyway. But I'd better get going, my flight leaves at six in the morning and I'm nowhere near done packing."

"Wait, before you go, do you recognise this symbol?" I grab one of the notepads behind the till and draw the circle with a line through it.

Sabine studies it with a frown on her face. "No, should I?"

I let out a loud sigh. "No, probably not."

"Why are you asking?"

I chew on my bottom lip, debating whether I should admit to being as suspicious of everything as I have been in the past few months.

"Aisha had this pin on her lapel when she tried to use blood magic on me," I say. "And then I saw it in one of the books you left, and again on the lapel of our rep at the Bureau."

"Hmm. I don't recognise it, but that doesn't mean anything. I'll keep an eye out," she says. "And so should you. I can't put my finger on why..."

"But something about this doesn't feel like a coincidence, I know."

She nods. "Exactly. Sometimes it's important to listen when something doesn't feel right."

"You've become so wise," I tease.

"It's the coffee. It fuels me."

"I know you think you're joking, but there's a good chance you're not." I smile at my best friend. "I'm going to miss you."

"You always do," she counters. "Though I warrant that you're going to miss me a little less this time." She nods towards the door that leads up to my flat.

I turn in time to see Azíl reappear and can sense how big the smile spreading across my face is.

I don't think there's any denying that she's right.

Chapter 9

I look up from making the coffee I'm currently working on to see Azíl masterfully handling the queue of customers. It's clear that he's a people person just from the way he takes to it. Just a couple of months ago, he was barely able to stay down here for ten minutes, and now he's managing entire shifts. I'm reasonably sure that if I left him to it, he'd be able to manage it on his own.

It makes me wonder what kind of career he'll pursue once we've broken his curse. I'm not naive enough to think that he'll want to stay at the coffee shop full time, not when there are so many more things that life is going to be able to offer him. Maybe he'll end up working with Sabine after all, though that will leave me rather lonely if they're both away.

Not that my inability to form new connections should stop either of them from following their dreams.

The bright ring of the telephone breaks through my thoughts. I reach out and pick it up, expecting to find one of my suppliers on the other end.

"Good morning, Cauldron Coffee Shop, how can I help you?" I ask.

"Is that Ms Reid?" A somewhat familiar voice asks, but I can't place it.

I glance back at Azíl to make sure he's all right, but he seems to be just fine.

"It is," I respond. "What is this about?"

"It's Wilfred from the Bureau for Witch and Warlock Affairs," the person on the other end says, his voice snapping into place in my mind.

"Ah, Wilfred, what can we do for you?" Why is he calling? So far all of the communications we've had with the department are via post or email, I don't see why he'd be contacting us in a different way all of a sudden, especially when I'm reasonably certain we've done everything we're supposed to already.

"I was wondering if you'd be able to bring Azíl's teapot into the Bureau."

A wave of cold sweeps through me as the words sink in. "What teapot?" I ask, reasonably sure that we avoided any mention of it anywhere in the paperwork or interviews.

Now I'm starting to feel as if I was right to be so nervous and protective over the situation.

"It is Bureau policy for us to inspect the cursed item," he says in a way that makes it seem almost plausible.

Emphasis on almost.

"I don't know what you're talking about, I'm sorry."

"Now, Ms Reid, why don't you put

Mr Amazigh on the phone and I'll discuss this with him."

"He will tell you the same thing as I am," I respond firmly. "We don't know what you're talking about. I apologise for wasting your time." I hang the phone up on the cradle and take a shaky breath.

"Are you all right, Willow?" Azíl asks, making me jump.

I press my hand against my chest, trying to calm my racing heart. "I'm sorry, you took me by surprise."

"Did you not have a good call?" He gestures to the phone.

I shake my head. "Wilfred called."

"Is there a problem with my application? I thought it had already been approved."

"It has," I assure him, not wanting him to worry about that, especially when he's been so excited about having an official identity and bank account.

"Why did he call?"

I glance around to make sure none of

the customers are paying any attention to us, but they all seem to be either seated with their drinks, or already halfway out of the door. "He wants us to bring your teapot to the Bureau," I whisper.

Azíl's eyes widen. "We can not do that."

"I know we can't." I take a deep breath. "Did you mention the teapot to him at all?"

He frowns. "I do not believe so, but there were many forms, I do not remember them all."

"Yeah, that's my problem too," I respond. "But I don't think we mentioned it, we were careful not to because of what it might mean." An uneasy feeling settles within me.

"We must have mentioned it, or how would he know?"

I let out a shaky breath. "I don't know." I look up at him, aware of the panic that's probably written all over my face. "That's what worries me."

He reaches out and takes my hand

in his. "It will be all right," he promises. "What did you tell him?"

I grimace. "That I had no idea what he was talking about."

Azíl chuckles. "How much did he insist?"

"Enough to make me think he really wants to see your teapot, not enough that I felt like it was an official request."

"Hmm, that is suspicious."

"Should we ask Mona and Daphne to bring it here?" I ask. "We don't have to keep it, but just so we can be sure that it's safe?"

"I thought you trusted them?"

"I do." Mostly because Sabine does, and because they helped us even though they didn't have to. "But they're not the only ones who are involved here. I'm worried about the people who are trying to recurse you. If they get their hands on the teapot..." I trail off, trying not to think too much about what would happen then.

"They would have to undo the sever first," he points out.

"I hadn't thought about that," I admit. "So they can't just summon you back to the teapot?"

He shakes his head. "Daphne gave me a book that had details of the sever spell that explained things. It said that the sever is making a wall between me and the teapot. If someone does something to the teapot, it will not affect me until the sever spell is either broken, or wears off."

"So we need to make sure that doesn't happen."

"The former will not," he assures me. "It said that it would include another spell to undo."

"And the latter?"

"Can happen."

"Okay, so we need to make sure it doesn't."

"I have no intention of letting it," he assures me. "I have too much to live for outside the teapot."

"And here was me thinking the

main problem with it would be that I'd be down a barista again."

He chuckles, the sound deep and reassuring, filling me with something other than worry and dread. "I would not want to do that to you. I see how you work too hard."

"If you think this is too hard, you should have seen me before you came along."

"I believe you are saying that I am good for you," he announces proudly.

A small snort escapes me. "I suppose I am, yes."

He nods. "I want to be good for you."

"That's sweet. I promise that I think you are, and that's all that matters." I go up on my toes and kiss his cheek. "But I'm going to message Mona and Daphne about the teapot. I'm going to worry if I don't."

"Then that is a good thing to do," he says.

"I'll get one of them to bring it after closing one night." I don't want anyone to see it by chance, not when Wilfred is calling and asking about it.

Something about the situation with the Bureau just doesn't seem right, and I can't quite put my finger on what it is. It certainly isn't the process itself, I checked everything against the government advice about the situation to make sure we were doing the right thing.

Which brings me back to Wilfred being the problem. The pin he wore every time we saw him isn't helping with that. I need to find out what the symbol means.

The bell rings and a customer approaches the counter.

"I will get it," Azíl says, already heading towards them and leaving me alone with my thoughts. I hope he's right and that we have nothing to worry about, but I can't help shake the feeling that something isn't right.

Chapter 10

I flick my wand towards the door, locking it tightly until Mona arrives. I don't want to risk someone entering the coffee shop who shouldn't be here.

"You are on edge," Azíl says.

I let out a loud sigh. "I can't help it. I just *feel* like something is going to go wrong, do you know what I mean?"

"I do." He turns to the water heater and makes us a pot of tea without me even asking him to.

I'm not sure exactly how it happened, but somehow freeing a cursed warlock from his teapot prison has ended up in the perfect live-in boyfriend. Even if Azíl doesn't fully understand the modern world, he's shown that he's quick to learn and slow to judge, which has made his transition a lot easier than it could have been.

"Here," he says, passing me a tea glass full of mint tea.

"Thank you." I smile at him so he knows how much I appreciate the gesture.

"The pattern on our glasses is starting to fade," he says, holding his up so I can see.

"That's because they're cheap. We can pick out some better ones together, if you want?" I suggest.

"I would like that. Where would we go?"

"I don't know," I admit. "I've never bought any tea glasses before these ones, and I only got them because you said you preferred drinking from them."

"I did not know that."

"Ah, that's because I never told you," I mumble.

"I appreciate it." He reaches out and pushes a strand of dark hair behind my ear. "Mona is here." He points to the door where the blonde witch is waving at us.

I flick my wand in her direction, unlocking it so she can enter, before locking up again. She doesn't even look behind her as the lock clicks into place, probably because she's fully aware of why I'm doing what I am. From the things she and Daphne have told us about their adventures in their first year at Grimalkin Academy, they're no strangers to making sure things that need to stay private do.

"Hey," she says.

"I have your tea," Azíl says, putting the takeaway cup full of chai tea latte down in front of the other witch.

"Oh, thanks, just what I need. And I have your teapot." She pulls it out of her bag and sets it on the counter between us. "It's a good thing you messaged me when you did, I was going to suggest I bring the pot back to you before I leave for the dig on Saturday."

"I didn't realise you were going too," I say.

She nods. "Sabine asked me to, I would have gone with the rest of the team, but I have an exam that I can't miss so I'm going later. Daphne and I were talking about how we thought it might be better if the teapot was here with you. We're sure the academy is secure, but it's still better to have two people looking over it than one."

I nod. "That makes sense." And honestly fills me with relief. Not just that we'll have the teapot with us where we'll be able to protect it, but also because it means both of the younger witches are sensible people. It's always reassuring to know those are around.

"Daphne is still at the academy though and will be working on the curse breaking when she can."

"Have you found anything yet?" Azíl asks.

Mona shakes her head. "We're still

trying to unravel a lot of the incantations on the outside of the pot. We have photos and magical maps of them, but there are thousands of years worth of spells on it, that's not easy to undo."

Azíl's face falls, but he covers his disappointment quickly. "Thank you for looking into it. I hope it does not take away too much time from your studies."

"Actually, it's good for that," Mona assures him. "We're doing a thesis on curse breaking and creating counter-curses to spells that have long since faded from time. Before this, it was mostly theoretical, or us studying curses that we created ourselves in a controlled environment. This gives us a much more practical understanding of the way we can actually apply our theories to the real world."

"I'm going to nod and pretend I understood that," I mutter.

Mona laughs lightly. "That's what one of my boyfriends does."

"Not the other two?"

She shakes her head. "They're more involved than Caspian is. Ryan's also coming on the dig with me, he has high hopes that we're going to find something that will help Azíl, though his suggestions about how are a little unorthodox."

"Is he suggesting using your kitten again?" I ask.

She chuckles. "More or less. Though I think his exact words were *take them all, that gives us eleven chances of accidentally discovering something*. He seems to have forgotten that while we did find a lot last time, we also nearly got trapped in a collapsing building."

"Probably best to avoid that," I say.

"Mmhmm."

"What happens if the sever starts to weaken while you are gone?" Azíl asks.

Mona frowns. "It shouldn't. They're not meant to last forever, but it should certainly last about six months tops."

"But if it does?" I prompt, not wanting to risk not knowing.

"If it does, Daphne can come and help you redo it," she says to me. "I think you'd probably be all right with just the two of you, but she can bring one of the guys with her too, that way you still have the power of three people."

I let out a sigh of relief. "And it's just a repeat of the last time?"

"The words are slightly different, but I'll email you a copy of the spell so you have it."

"Thank you, we appreciate it," I tell her. "I know it might seem like I'm worrying more than I should..."

"Not at all. I've been cursed, I know how stressful it is," she reminds me. "Anyway, I should get going, but if there's anything else you need, you know how to reach me."

"Thank you, Mona," Azíl says with a dip of his head.

"Anytime. Would you mind getting the door for me, Willow?"

I nod and send a quick spell in the direction of the door, letting it swing open for her and not just unlock.

She waves goodbye and I close the door behind her, leaving us in privacy once more.

I stare at the teapot, not knowing what to do with it now it's back. I haven't spent much time around it since the sever spell, but even from this distance, I can tell that it's different.

I reach out and touch it. Nothing comes from it, not like when Azíl was connected to it and I could feel his emotions.

"I wish Spooky was around to tell me what she thought about it," I admit.

"She will be back," Azíl promises. "Her owner is probably keeping her inside until her foot is healed."

"I know. But I still miss her."

He reaches out and pulls me to him, kissing the top of my head. "She misses you too."

"You don't know that," I point out.

"I know I would miss you if I was

kept away. It is something I have thought about many times in recent weeks. I used to believe that the worst thing about having my curse placed on me again and again was that I never got to actively be a part of life that went on around me. But it is different now. The worst thing would not be leaving life behind, but leaving you, and knowing that you would be sad."

"I'd be more than sad," I admit, reaching up to touch his cheek. "But you have to know that if that happens and you do end up stuck in your teapot again, I won't stop looking for you until I find you."

"You can not. You will waste your life."

"No. I won't. If the worst happens, I will find you, I am sure of it."

"I hope you are right."

"Your future is safe with me," I promise. I meet his gaze, hoping he can see how much I mean the words, and how important it is to me that he understands.

"I know. You have always felt safe to me."

He leans in and presses his lips against mine, kissing me so softly that I can feel all of the emotions he's trying to convey.

I wrap my arms around his neck and deepen the kiss, making sure he can sense my feelings to the same extent. Because no one has made me feel the way I do about him before, and I'm determined not to let anything take those feelings from me, especially not by cursing him to another hundred years trapped in his teapot.

Not while I'm still living and breathing.

We break apart and he smiles at me. "I am going to put the teapot back in its safe space."

I nod. "I just need to turn the coffee machine off now it's finished cleaning, then I'll be up. We can watch a movie or something?"

"The latest episode of *Fang Me* is on," he says with an impish grin.

"Fine, we can watch *Fang Me*, but if I get addicted to it too, I'm going to blame you."

"I take no responsibility for that."

I shake my head in amusement, already resigned to the fact I'm probably going to end up invested in all of his shows. "I'll see you upstairs."

He grabs the teapot and heads in the direction of the door, stopping and turning to smile at me before he goes up.

My heart skips a beat and I let out a long drawn-out sigh. It would be easy to be angry that he's complicated my life, but how can I be when my life is all the better for meeting him.

Chapter 11

"What do you want to eat tonight?" I ask as I enter the living room, only to stop in my tracks at the sight of Azíl sitting on the sofa with the teapot on the coffee table in front of him and a sad expression on his face.

Without saying a word, I head over and sit down next to him, taking his hand in mine and entwining our fingers.

I wish I had a way of asking what's on his mind without it sounding like a woefully inadequate question. Something is clearly bothering him, and I hate that I don't know what it is.

"Do you want me to put it away?" I ask, gesturing to the teapot with my free hand.

"No." His voice cracks as he says the word. "I was just having a moment."

"Do you want to talk about it?"

"Would you drop the subject if I say no?"

"Of course."

"Even if you are curious?" he checks.

I chuckle dryly. "Even if I'm curious," I confirm. "But wanting to know doesn't give me the right to press you on something you don't want to talk about."

He smiles sadly. "I do wish to talk about it."

"But?"

"I do not know what it is I want to talk about."

"Ah, that problem."

"It is a common one?" Hope lights up his face.

I nod. "Sometimes, people get sad

just because they're sad. Nothing has to happen to cause it. And if you want to talk about it, then I guess we'll start with the basics. Are you hungry?"

He frowns. "No. What has that got to do with sad?"

"It's something my dad taught me. If you're feeling an intense emotion, check that you're not hungry or tired first."

"That is good advice."

"I agree. So are you tired or hungry?" I ask.

He closes his eyes and considers for a moment. "I do not believe so."

"That's a good start. When did you start feeling sad?"

"I came upstairs and the teapot felt heavy, so I put it down, and then I looked at it and I felt very sad."

"Okay, so it's the teapot."

"I do not want it to be the teapot," Azíl admits. "But I believe you are right."

"I'm not surprised. I feel a little sad when I look at the teapot," I say. "I think about all of the time you spent inside there alone and it fills me with sadness and anger that you were there for so long."

"It was not so bad. I did not feel time passing the same way I do now."

"Which is a good thing, but it doesn't change the way I feel."

"I do not mind too much. I like the world I have found myself in. There are lots of things that I think suit me about it."

"Like the fact you can order food to the door and you don't have to cook it yourself?" I half-tease.

"That is an excellent advantage," he agrees. "But there is more to it. No one questions that I am friends with Sabine, or that I live here with you, those things just *are*. I like that. And I like being able to watch TV. I always liked stories, but it felt like something was missing, I think that it was the pictures you have to go with them."

"We should try you on comics," I

say, making a mental note to pick one out for him.

"I like that there is more variety of food, especially food that comes to the door. And drinks."

"Maybe you just like choice," I suggest, half-joking, but definitely sensing a common theme in the things he's saying.

He cocks his head to the side and contemplates it. "I believe you are right. I like choice. My time did not allow me much choice. And it afforded my friend even less choice."

"I'm sorry."

"It is not your fault," he responds. "Nor is it really mine."

"It isn't," I agree.

"I would do it all again," he says. "Even knowing that I would end up cursed and alone for a long time. I would have done what she asked me to."

"I'm sure she was very grateful for what you did," I respond, recalling his story of the girl who was forced to marry and the disfigurement he gave her at her own request. "Not many people would do that, even now."

"She would like you," he says, a hint of sadness in his voice. "Sometimes, I am sad that you will never get to meet."

"We might in the next life," I assure him, then frown. "Do you believe in the next life?"

"I am not sure," he admits. "My people believed in the afterlife, but I do not know if I do. But perhaps that is because I spent so long unable to die. In a few years, I may feel differently."

"There are a lot more religions for you to choose from now," I point out. "You can find the one that suits you. Not all of them believe in an afterlife."

"I think I would like that."

"So are you sad because of the past?"

He sighs. "I believe I am sad because I am happy."

"Ah."

"Does that make sense to you?"

I nod. "You were cursed because you were being punished. Maybe a part of you believes that you should be punished for what you did, even if you think that it was morally right. But now, you're having to come to terms with the fact that your curse might not be forever, and that you have a chance to be happy and live for yourself. And maybe there's a little bit of guilt in there too that the chief's daughter doesn't have the same chance at life as you now have."

"You are very observant."

"I've heard a lot of heart-to-hearts. It comes with the territory of running a coffee shop. It gives me some insight into these things."

"I believe I have heard some of these heart-to-hearts too. They would be like this conversation, right?"

"Yes." I stroke my thumb over the back of his hand almost absentmind-edly, enjoying the casual contact, as well as the contrast between our different skin colours, there's something beautiful about it that I can't put into words.

"I want to be happy," he says.

"I want that too."

"You make me happy."

I smile at him. "I'm glad. But your happiness can't solely rest on me. You need to find other things that make you happy too. Like your shows, your job, anything you want, really."

"My job?"

I nod. "You seem to like working at the coffee shop, but is that what *you* want to do? I know it's best for now, but once your curse is properly broken, you'll just be a normal warlock and you can do anything you want to. You could go and study at one of the academies to get some qualifications, or you could train for a vocation."

"I could choose a job?" he echoes.

I nod. "It's not quite as easy as that. We'll need to make sure you're qualified for it, and then there'll be preparing for interviews, and you know what, we should worry about that part later. But you should think about what you want to do."

"Can I decide to stay at the coffee shop?" he asks.

"You can, if that's what you want."

"Perhaps there are too many choices in this world."

I let out a small laugh. "You wouldn't be the first person to say that."

"I feel a little better," he says.

"Good, I'm glad. Shall I put the teapot away?"

He nods. "Will you put strong spells around it, to keep it safe? I do not want to carry it around with us all the time."

"Of course." I lean in and kiss his cheek. "I'll put it in the safe."

I get to my feet and pick up the teapot, taking it into the small room I sometimes use as an office. Not that I use it very often, why would I when I have a fancy coffee machine downstairs?

I put in the combination, making a note to tell Azíl it so he doesn't feel like

I'm locking the teapot away from him. I put it inside and relock the door.

That will deal with any potential human thieves, but Azíl's suggestion of some extra protection isn't a bad one. I pull out my wand and start to cast a series of intricate spells that should ward off most people. Only those who are a lot more powerful than me should be able to get through without knowing exactly which ones I've used.

I step back and admire my handi-work. Hopefully, it will be enough. But I doubt they'll be needed.

The only two people who know where the teapot is are in this flat. Nothing is going to happen to it while it's locked up tightly.

Chapter 12

The warm evening air is a pleasant surprise after the cold snap we've been having. I slip my arm through Azíl's and lean into him, enjoying the simplicity of being outside the coffee shop with no other purpose than enjoying ourselves.

"You still haven't told me where we're going," I say.

"That is because it is a surprise," Azíl responds.

"Please?"

He chuckles, the hearty sound that warms my heart. "You do not have to wait to find out, we are here." He gestures to the restaurant in front of us.

The ornate writing on the front of the building spells out the name *Pierre Blanche* and I let out a small gasp of surprise. "But..."

"It is your favourite restaurant in the town," he says.

"It is. But how did you know?"

"I asked Sabine where I should take you if I wanted it to be special."

"Oh, Azíl." I lean in and kiss his cheek.

"Why have we not been here before if it is your favourite?"

"Because it's expensive."

"Then it is good that you are not paying."

I can tell there's no point arguing with him, and a large part of me doesn't want to. It's such a sweet thing for him to do. Not because he's brought me somewhere fancy, but because he's gone to the trouble of asking Sabine where to take me, and keeping it all a surprise.

He pulls open the door for me and lets me step inside.

"Good evening," a waiter says as we step inside.

"I have a booking," Azíl says.

"Very good, sir. What name would that be under?"

"Amazigh," he responds, and I can hear the pride in his voice as he says his new surname. I wonder if that's also part of why he chose a fancy restaurant.

"For two?"

"Yes," Azíl confirms.

"Very good, sir. Your table will be ready in ten minutes, if you would like to wait at the bar until then." He gestures for us to go around to the left.

"Thank you." Azíl dips his head to him and leads me around to the other side. "What do we do here?" he whispers.

"We get a drink," I respond, gesturing for the bartender. "Hi, I'd like a dry white wine, please."

"Of course, ma'am, and for you, sir?" he asks Azíl.

He stares with his eyes wide.

"A fruity red for him, please," I say, realising that he needs saving.

"Thank you," Azíl says when the man has gone to get our wine. "But I do not know what you ordered for me."

"Red wine," I respond. "I thought you would prefer it to white."

"I do not believe I have had either. I suspect it will not taste like the wine I have had before."

"No, probably not."

The bartender returns with our drinks and places them down in front of us. "Would you like the drinks added to your table?"

"No, I would like to pay now," Azíl announces, already pulling out his new bank card.

I smother my amusement, but mostly because I know it'll only raise questions from the bartender.

Confusion crosses the man's face at

the slightly strange request, but he goes to get the card machine anyway.

"What do I do now?" Azíl asks.

"You just need to touch your card to the screen when he says so."

Azíl frowns. "Just touch it?"

I nod. "When it beeps, you've paid."

"Ah."

The bartender returns and holds out the card reader for Azíl.

Slowly, he touches his card to the screen. I wait with a little bit of nervousness fluttering within me. I know there's money in his account, I put it there as his wages from working at the coffee shop, but a part of me is still worried that it's going to decline.

I don't relax until the machine beeps, signalling its success.

Azíl's face lights up. "Thank you," he says to the confused bartender.

There's no keeping the smile off my face.

"Cheers," I say, holding my glass to

him. "A toast to paying for something for the first time."

The look on his face tells me everything I need to know.

"You say cheers and clink your glass to mine," I explain. "It's a toast, just something you do when you're celebrating something."

"Ah, I see." He leans his glass forward and gently clinks it against mine. "Cheers."

"What would you do when you shared a drink with someone?" I take a sip of my wine.

"We would tell stories," he responds. "Or swap knowledge. Sometimes we would have a feast to celebrate someone's success if it was very great."

"That sounds nice."

"Sometimes it was, sometimes it got in the way of other important work."

"Ah, so things haven't really changed much, then," I joke.

"Do social engagements still get in the way?"

"Very much so for people who prefer to keep to themselves. Not at all for those who enjoy being around lots of people," I respond.

He nods and takes a sip of his wine. "Mmm, I like this."

"Would you like to try white wine?" I ask, offering him my glass.

"I would." He sets his glass down and takes mine from me, letting his fingers brush against mine as he does.

My breathing hitches at the brief contact. We touch all the time but I still love the way it feels. And sometimes, I think I like the reminder that he's still here.

Still solid.

He takes a sip of my wine and wrinkles his nose. "I prefer the red." He hands it back to me.

"I thought you might. There are some sweeter white wines that I think you might like though. And some dessert wines."

"There are lots of choices for

wine." There's a twinkle in his eyes as he says it.

"You do like choice."

"It is my second favourite thing in the modern world."

"Oh? What is your favourite?"

"That is a hard one, it has to be a choice between you and cake." There's a playful hint in his voice that keeps me smiling.

"I'd choose cake," I tease.

"But I am lucky, I do not have to choose. And your coffee shop has both."

"You're not wrong there," I agree.

The waiter approaches us, cutting our conversation short. "Mr Amazigh, your table is ready now. If you would like to follow me." He gestures towards the main restaurant.

Azíl holds his arm out to me and I slip my arm through, allowing him to lead me into the dining room.

It's barely getting started, but I think this is going to be my favourite date ever.

Chapter 13

I let out a light laugh as we turn back onto our street, leaning against Azíl's shoulder and feeling buoyed up by how fun our evening together has been.

"Thank you for dinner," I say to him.

"You have got me plenty of dinners."

"I know, but that's what you're supposed to say when someone has paid for your meal."

"Ah, you are speaking of dating rules."

I chuckle. "Not just dating in this

case. You'd say it to anyone who paid for your food."

"I will make sure to remember that."

"But if you want to talk about dating conventions, here's my door," I say with a slightly flirtatious note in my voice. "Would you like to come in for some coffee?"

"Is that metaphorical coffee, or real coffee?" he asks.

A small laugh escapes me. "You're not supposed to ask."

"Then we shall have both," he announces.

I shake my head in amusement and reach for my wand to undo the locking spells, only to realise that I can't see any trace of them.

I reach out and push on the door, watching it swing open without any input from me. "I thought I locked the door," I whisper, horror running through me.

"You did. I watched you do it," Azíl says. "And you put a spell on it too."

"So why is the door open?"

"I do not know," he responds needlessly.

Dread sits in the pit of my stomach. Somehow, I know what we're going to find inside. The coffee shop equipment is expensive, but difficult to manage to steal, especially given that whoever did this has long gone. And I doubt they'll have broken in for the money, not when there's a jewellery store just a few doors down, and their comings and goings are much easier to predict than ours.

"Can you do a spell to trace their footsteps?" Azíl asks.

I nod. "Is that something you used to do?"

"I did not do it personally, but I knew a few warlocks who used it often."

I lift my wand and give it a flick, summoning the spell from within me. The magic shoots out of the wand and illuminates the area around the door's lock, revealing what I already feared to be true.

Another witch or warlock has been here, and they're more powerful than I am.

"Ready?" I ask Azíl.

"No," he responds.

"Me neither." I reach out and push the door open, following the magical trace inside. It goes straight past the till and the expensive equipment, only confirming my suspicions about what this is going to be about.

I hope the spells I put on the safe have held, but I suspect we're about to discover that's not true. I knew we should have taken the teapot with us, even if it isn't what Azíl wants.

I lock the door behind us, but don't break the growing silence as we follow the trail of magic to the flat door. Whoever did this hasn't even bothered to pretend they're up to something else. I'm not sure if they just assumed that we'd connect the dots, or if they don't care.

I suppose it'll depend on what things look like inside.

Azíl pushes the door to the flat open, which means they've also managed to dismantle the locks I put in place there. I'm going to need to have someone come and place some wards in the morning, otherwise, we're never going to be able to sleep soundly here again.

I suck in a deep breath as I take in the sight of the flat. Things are strewn everywhere, and the sofa has clearly been knifed in an attempt to uncover a hiding place.

I move slowly as I take it in, trying not to let the tears welling up in my eyes burst free. The only room that doesn't seem to be affected is Sabine's. No doubt her necromancer magic proved too difficult for them to undo. I should have thought of that and asked her if we could keep the teapot in there.

But I suspect it's too late for that.

I come to a stop in front of the

door to the office, too scared of what I'm going to find to go in alone.

Azíl slips his hand into mine and gives it a squeeze. "Together?" he asks.

I nod, certain that he's come to the same conclusion as I have about what we're going to find.

Even though I already knew what we were going to find when we stepped inside, horror and shock still rush through me as we enter and find the safe hanging open, my protection spells completely destroyed by whoever came inside.

"Azíl, I'm so sorry," I whisper. "I can't believe I let this happen." I can't take my eyes off the empty safe.

He steps in front of me so he's obstructing my view. "This is not your fault," he says firmly.

"But..."

He shakes his head. "It is not your fault, Willow. You did nothing wrong."

"I'm the one whose protection spells weren't good enough."

"I believe you used the strongest ones you know."

"I did."

"Then there is nothing for you to be sorry about," he repeats. "You did nothing wrong."

"Maybe we should have left the teapot at the academy after all."

"Maybe," he responds. "Or it could have been stolen from there too."

"How are you not scared right now?" I ask.

"I am terrified," he responds. "I do not want to go back into the teapot. I do not want to leave you. But right now, we need to think, and panicking will not achieve that."

I take a deep breath and then let it out slowly. "You're right. So, what do we do?"

"We call your law-keepers," he points out. "Someone has broken into our home, they may be able to do something about it."

"That's a good point. Let's do that," I say. "It's going to be okay, right?"

He nods. "They must have had the teapot for a few hours at least, and I am not inside it," he points out.

"Okay, so long as you're here, it's good. We just have to hope that they..." I trail off.

"Willow?"

"What if they placed a bug in the flat?"

"A bug? I do not know what this means?"

"Oh, sorry. A bug is a listening device, so they can hear what we're talking about," I explain.

"Do you have a spell that will detect them?" he asks.

"Yes, but I'm not sure what good it will do if they're stronger than me magically." Which they clearly are.

"What about asking someone who is stronger than you to do the spell?"

"That could work. We could ask Daphne?" I don't know that the younger witch is more powerful than me for certain, but I know her friend is.

And even if she isn't, we could combine our powers.

"Let us start by making sure the flat is secure," he says. "And then we will work out what to do next."

I nod. "Okay."

"And Willow?"

"Yes?"

"It is going to be all right," he promises.

"How can you know that for sure?"

The smile he gives me is almost enough to reassure me. "Because I have faith in us, and you should too."

I hope he isn't misplacing it. And that we're going to be able to figure this out before it's too late.

▭

Thank you for reading *Peppermint Tea And Nothing Is Free*, I hope you enjoyed it! If you want to continue the series (which I promise will have a happy ending for the Spooky plotline too!), you can in *Cinnamon Cocoa And Far To*

Go: http://books2read.com/
cinnamoncocoaandfartogo

If you want to read about Azíl and Willow's date from Azíl's point of view, you can here: https://books.authorlauragreenwood.co.uk/te9bdbxzdu

Author Note

Thank you for reading *Peppermint Tea And Nothing Is Free*, I hope you enjoyed it!

This isn't the end of the *Cauldron Coffee Shop* series, and there is plenty more to come. When I originally started the series, I did intend for it to be a three-book one, ending with *Peppermint Tea And Nothing Is Free* (this book). But when it came to actually writing it, I realised that there was no way I was going to be able to get everything in, especially not after I'd met Willow and Azíl as characters. In some respects, they've gone faster than in my original plot, but in others, they've gone a little slower. It's been a fun ride so far, and I hope you'll join me for the rest of it!

If you're wondering about the surname Azíl picked, Amazigh is (allegedly) the word that the Berbers (the native Moroccans from around the time Azíl was cursed) used to refer to themselves, though there has been debate about the translation as the Berber language remains a mystery to historians. However, the proposed meaning of the term was just too perfect for Azíl and his story not to use it. Because the language isn't well documented or understood, it wasn't possible for me to include it in the story, even when Azíl is talking in his native tongue.

A note on the Spooky plotline: it isn't over, and I promise it will end happily for everyone involved (Spooky included). I wouldn't normally include a spoiler like this so far from the end of the series, but I know that pets can be a difficult subject for many people, so I feel that it is necessary.

If you're wondering about Mona's history as the victim of a curse, then you can follow her in the first part of the *Grimalkin Academy* series (the second part follows Daphne) where she deals with magically appearing kittens whenever she tries to cast a spell. Her time at the dig where she and Ryan found the teapot is also the plotline of *This Time Is Trouble* (her happy ever after book!). And if you haven't read Sabine and Sawyer's story, *Unfortunate Decrees And Iced Coffees*, yet, then I highly recommend doing so - Sawyer will appear a little more in the next book! And, while Willow's cousins didn't appear in this book, they do have their own series called *Broomstick Bakery*, which sees each of the siblings find romance.

If you want to keep up to date with new releases and other news, you can join my Facebook Reader Group or mailing list.

Stay safe & happy reading!

- Laura

Get a free Cauldron
Coffee Shop Story

**CAn investigation into a
mysterious stone leads a
necromancer and a warlock
closer together.**

When necromancer archaeologist,
Sabine, is asked to supervise an
excavation of the mysterious Humber
Stone, she can't resist the challenge.

But when she arrives and discovers her
warlock ex is intent on stopping the
dig, she realises it may be a harder task
than she first thought.

The excavation may be plagued by the bad luck brought about by the stone, but at least things aren't quite so bad for Sabine's love life…

-

Unfortunate Decrees and Iced Coffees is a companion story of the Cauldron Coffee Shop urban fantasy series. It includes a stubborn necromancer archeologist, a mysterious stone, a handsome warlock, and a second chance romantic subplot.

If you love cozy urban fantasy, coffee shop settings, low-stakes adventures, cat familiars, and a warm and fuzzy feeling vibe, start the Cauldron Coffee Shops series with Pumpkin Spice And All Things Nice.

You can get your free copy of Unfortunate Decrees and Iced Coffees here: https://books. authorlauragreenwood.co.uk/sabine

Also by Laura Greenwood

You can find out more about each of my
series on my website.

- The Apprentice Of Anubis: an
  urban fantasy series set in an
  alternative world where the
  Ancient Egyptian Empire
  never fell. It follows a new
  apprentice to the temple of
  Anubis as she learns about her
  new role.
- Forgotten Gods: a paranormal
  adventure romance series
  inspired by Egyptian
  mythology. Each book follows
  a different Ancient Egyptian
  goddess.
- Jinx Paranormal Dating
  Agency: a paranormal
  romance series based on
  worldwide mythology where
  paranormals and deities take
  part in events organised by the

Jinx Dating Agency. Each book follows a different couple.

- House Of Blood And Roses: a vampire romantasy series following a heroine who discovers she's a vampire noble and has to navigate a world full of politics, betrayal, and blood lust.
- Amethyst's Wand Shop Mysteries (with Arizona Tape): an urban fantasy murder mystery series following a witch who teams up with a detective to solve murders. Each book includes a different murder.
- Scales Of Justice: an urban fantasy following a thief who accidentally becomes the newest apprentice of the goddess of truth.
- Purple Oak Oasis (with Ariana Jade): a cozy fantasy romance series with unusual magic. Each book follows a different couple.
- Falhaven Castle: a cozy fantasy romance series following a princess who just wants to

bake, a slow burn friends-to-lovers romance, and an adorable baking dragon.

- Speed Dating With The Denizens Of The Underworld (shared world): a paranormal romance shared world based on mythology from around the world. Each book follows a different couple.
- Blackthorn Academy For Supernaturals (shared world): a paranormal monster romance shared world based at Blackthorn Academy. Each book follows a different couple.

You can find a complete list of all my books on my website:

https://books.authorlauragreenwood.co.uk/book-list

Signed Paperback & Merchandise:

You can find signed paperbacks, hardcovers, and merchandise based on my series (including stickers, magnets, face masks, and more!) via my website:

https://books.authorlauragreenwood.co.uk/shop

About Laura Greenwood

Laura is a USA Today Bestselling Author of paranormal romance, urban fantasy, and fantasy romance. When she's not writing, she drinks a lot of tea, tries to resist French macarons, and works towards a diploma in Egyptology. She lives in the UK, where most of her books are set. Laura specialises in quick reads, with healthy relationships and consent-positive moments regardless of if she's writing light-hearted romance, mythology-heavy urban fantasy, or anything in between.

Follow Laura Greenwood

- Website: www.authorlaura-greenwood.co.uk
- Mailing List: https://books.

authorlauragreenwood.co.
uk/newsletter

- Facebook Group: http://
  facebook.com/groups/
  theparanormalcouncil
- Discord Server: https://
  discord.gg/W6zExZkUG6
- Facebook Page: http://
  facebook.com/
  authorlauragreenwood
- Bookbub: https://www.
  bookbub.com/authors/
  laura-greenwood

www.ingramcontent.com/pod-product-compliance
Lightning Source LLC
Chambersburg PA
CBHW020930160726
47993CB00005B/2221